GOODNIGHT NOBODY

and other haunted bedtime stories

Pauline Chow

Ghastly Goings-On Press

Copyright © 2024 by Pauline Chow
All rights reserved.
ISBN-13: 978-1-964733-00-5

No part of this publication may be reproduced, distributed, or transmitted in any form or by any means, including photocopying, recording, or other electronic or mechanical methods, without the prior written permission of the publisher, except as permitted by U.S. copyright law. For permission requests, contact the author, Pauline Chow.

The story, all names, characters, and incidents portrayed in this production are fictitious. No identification with actual persons (living or deceased), places, buildings, and products are intended or should be inferred.

Cover Art & Illustrations by Andrew Machulski
Fun Edition 2024

To Andrew:

My companion on many sleepless nights

Goodnight Nobody	1
A Wicked Spice	8
Red's Offerings	11
Listen, Before It's Too Late	28
On the Isle of the Wild	31
The Vegetarian	35
The Thing About Cheese	44
Born of the Blood Moon	47
Author Notes	54
About Author	56

GOODNIGHT NOBODY

In the great green room, Grandma's fingers ache, crafting from the last skein a new future. Needles click and clack. The scent of the crackling fire and cinnamon lingers. Seconds tick on the clock. A breeze sings as her grandchild taps the bedpost. The child yawns as an almost round moon beckons through the glass. Time crescendos.

Grandma rocks back and forth praying for bountiful harvests, good health, and for the village to endure in the divine. She must not falter on tonight's deadline.

"Old lady, Nobody is coming," says the sleepy child in striped pajamas whose birth

GOODNIGHT NOBODY

defied ancient rites.

Grandma's wrists stiffen, holding the count of the stitches. A bitter aftertaste coats her tongue from a cup of chicory and clover. She braids the final sleeve of a thousand limbed sweater, started before her lifetime. Her daughter had been unable to finish.

"Young one, sleep," huffs the lady. Cold breath circles the knit. The fire simmers on the final log, but her hands keeps spinning.

"I want to see the stars." Her grandchild pouts in curiosity, slithering over the blanket. Shadows animate the pictures on the walls. Snakes intertwining a shaft. A cow bounds over stars.

Grandma shutters, crossing and looping the threads as moonlight highlights a gold streak in the child's hair. "See it tomorrow," she says with unease.

The child wiggles, showing a sly smile.

"Children must sleep tonight. Do you remember why?"

GOODNIGHT NOBODY

"Gran, I do." The words come light. "But you are the Keeper, so I will be safe during the festival."

Grandma shakes her head. She couldn't shelter her own daughter. "The Black Goat Mother cannot know of your existence. Her thousand ewes love the taste of children. So, hush." She fastens the yarn ends and speaks the fable once more:

Legends say our village wanted a hundred sons. A shroud was offered to the Mother of the Wood, one of the many old gods, as a plea for fertility. Wishes for strength, boldness, and wealth uttered from the mouth of fools. They offered a mat of virgin hair weaved in gold. The old leader, a man with a gray beard and broad sword, carried this disillusioned request into the forest. The Mother meet him and never let him go. She wanted more, and so after fathering her atrocities, his bones were thrown into a cavern.

Yet, the shroud offering brought life, filling every womb. Men rejoiced, mourning the loss of the leader and celebrating future

GOODNIGHT NOBODY

masculine heirs. In their dreams, anticipated glories abound from the far corners of the world.

But one-by-one the midwives simpered, because each mother birthed a girl. By attrition and time, males expired. Now, an appointed female in each generation offers a blessing or a bit of their flesh. The Mother and her children hunger for wrought sacrifices.

The child peers out of the window. "I wonder if my mom is still out there."

"Hush. You will appreciate the pact one day. It's late, say goodnight to the toy house, comb and brush, and uneaten mush." Twisting and stretching, the sacred shroud is nearly complete.

The child's eyes grow heavy with the nightly spell. Bleating noises clusters beyond the fields. Trees shake. Grandma ties the final knot.

She inspects decades of labor, rows like tree rings, mapping lives within the binds and pearls. Her gnarled fingers slide across the section by her daughter, who had been taken by the Mother's kids outside of the ancient covenant.

"Goodnight, my little mouse," whispers Grandma, sheathing the broad sword and dragging the shroud down the path. Red candles light the way with shrines hoping for the old woman's return. Chanting floats from the village square as hooves stomp in the distance. Someone must bear the consequences for broken rules.

When the world is quiet, Grandma inhales the thickening air. A decaying must singes the hairs in her nostrils. Trees are more twisted and overgrown in the valley. Insects screech, not hum. Wolves snarl instead of howl. The smell of decay stings her eyes. She hears the footfall of a small animal. She extends the extends arms in a field, invoking the ceremony.

Black Goat Mother, these offerings are to unburden your woes.
May we live in the Divine.
May we thrive in the feminine.
May the Darkness be satisfied.

GOODNIGHT NOBODY

"Goodnight Nobody," she calls upon the Black Goat Mother. Grandma is ready. A faint *maa maa* rattles in the distance.

Bushes rustle as a chortling creature jumps out. Grandma steps back. A flash of black and white confirms this is her grandchild, not a ravenous goat kid. Tightness grips the old lady's chest as she grabs the hand of the intruder.

But it's too late. A four-legged kid, the size of a bear cub, blocks the return route. With distended vertical red eyes, it bares sharp teeth. Grandma's back seizes as she draws the sword. Her grandchild walks towards the unfamiliar.

Her little mouse is not scared, standing face-to-face with a salivating beast. It's breath smells of soured milk and cut grass. She reaches for the kid's wet snout.

Grandma watches a shadow lurk at the tree line. Goosebumps feather her arms. The Black Mother's limbs fill the sleeves. Salvia drips from its thousand mouths, gnashing in delight.

GOODNIGHT NOBODY

High-pitched screams rips into the night. The Mother recoils as the moon shines from its apex.

The kid hits the ground with a loud thud. Its body convulsing. Human handprints are seared into its fur.

Her grandchild helps Grandma to her feet. "It wanted to play." The grandchild extends blooded hands.

Lifting the sword, the old lady declares: "You're the divine, a neuter, the merging of the masculine and feminine. We broke the rules first. Darkness summons a new sacrifice."

A WICKED SPICE

Gretel hated chewing. She wrestled with hunger, her life's twisting force. Abandoned by her father when the pantry was bare, she and her brother fretted over breadcrumbs. Confections lured her empty stomach into a gingerbread house.

She sucked on a cigarette, smoldering her appetite with charred tobacco and paper. Sot tasted better than the guilt of burnt flesh. Forbidden flavors never dulled.

The rumors weren't true. Her brother hadn't escaped.

More children frolicked into the woods and filled their bellies on candies laid out by

A WICKED SPICE

a ravenous landlord: pay with your body or your innocence.

    Hunger was a wicked spice

RED'S OFFERINGS

"I can eat you up," shouted a young man over the music.

"You will do." Meredith peered into his eyes. She was a glutton for eagerness, gliding her fingers down his fifty percent cotton and fifty percent polyester t-shirt. A tuft of hair peaked from v-neck collar. The mustard color reminded Meredith of a rug in her Popo's house. She missed her mother's mother very much.

He pressed his sweaty body into hers, breathing out liquored words. As the DJ transitioned to a hard bass, drunk people jostled her. She giggled and twirled a red

GOODNIGHT NOBODY

scarf. Pointing at the bar, she mouthed *drink*. The man took her hand, allowing Meredith to drag him through the crowd. In a lap dog sort of way, he was cute.

The bar was crowded. She gulped down another tonic. Gnawing at the sprig of thyme, she tried not to look him directly in the eyes. Sap stuck to the roof of her mouth. "What's your name?"

"Georg….g." His head swayed. "You smell like a campfire."

"Camping?" The words stuck to her teeth. She squeezed his bicep. He had muscles for doing work, not solely for looking pretty.

"We…my family…go…" He closed his eyes and smiled as if reliving a thought. "I can…take…"

An idea jostled in Meredith's mind. George was outdoorsy, not the typical find in a sea of designer jeans. An idea surged in her mind. This could be the end. As he rocked on his heels, George tipped too far back.

RED'S OFFERINGS

Her hand shot out, grabbing his collar. Whiskey sloshed onto her dress. "Damn it." Sticky liquid dripped into her bra. George's eyes glazed over. She squinted at this specimen. Today wasn't right. He wasn't ready. She had to prepare.

Licking her lips, she slipped her phone number into his pocket. She pressed her lips onto his, hoping they would meet again.

He hiccupped. "You taste like cinnamon."

To Meredith, he tasted like freedom.

***

Next time, Meredith skipped the throbbing lights and loud music. Finding a more conducive environment for seduction.

Luke parked his open top convertible in the rocky driveway. "Why didn't we go to my apartment?" He frowned, combing out his blond waves. The strands falling through his fingers.

Meredith picked him up at a jazz club furnished with velvety seats.

GOODNIGHT NOBODY

"The stars," she tilted her hair back, exposing her slender neck. He leaned in, kissed a line along her flesh. "I had to show you the sky." He smelled of manufactured cologne, musky without a purpose.

"It's perfect," he mumbled, not noticing a shadow shifting in the cabin window. He tugged on the red scarf around her head.

She pushed away his hand, readjusting her clothes. "I didn't tell you. Grandma lives in this house."

"Uh. Why is this weird?" Suspicion flashed in Luke's expression. He glided his tongue across sparkling teeth.

"She'll be interested in you, but…" Meredith nuzzled into the nape of Luke's neck. She touched the inside of his leg, and he groaned.

"What harm can an old lady do?" he said. Even if he had asked, she wasn't in the mood to tell him.

***

RED'S OFFERINGS

Later, Meredith checked her phone in her sleeping bag. Grandma's house had become dreadful, so she slept outside. Her heart fluttered.

"It's George. I found your phone number. Guess I should have done laundry sooner? [::smiley face with tongue::] How are you?"

"I am great. Glad you msg." She replied in a flash. He had an earthy scent and strong hands. Since their encounter, she practiced holding her breath and sharpen a knife.

Over the weeks, Meredith texted with George. Sharing tidbits of her story, but not everything:

She lived in the woods without her parents.

Only visiting the city when grandma needed things.

She enjoyed fairytales — tradition and ones with a modern twist.

High rises, grid-planned streets, and traffic stressed her the F out.

GOODNIGHT NOBODY

Her favorite color was red.

He offered to visit, sharing details about his past trips. He had camped in the mountains and canoed down rivers. While he was not an avid hunter, he had dressed a dozen or so does. If the hands and feet are removed, then the rest of the fur just glides off.

"Have you ever seen [::wolf::]?" Meredith inserted an animal emoji instead of the word.

"Zoo and books. Aren't they extinct?"

"Endangered." She corrected his knowledge of the local predators.

"Is there deer in your area?"

"Not really." Meredith couldn't remember the last time a gentle four-legged survived in her woods.

"Predators need a healthy food supply."

"I know." She touched the scarf wrapped around her neck.

RED'S OFFERINGS

"It'll be fun," he said with a heart emoji.

She replied with a thumbs up. If only her life was so easy.

"Will I meet grandmother?"

"Grandma is not all together." Meredith wanted George and her to have a different fate.

***

Meredith arranged a date with George at a cafe. Concrete sidewalks and asphalt streets absorbed the sun's heat. Grim clung to her skin. She dreaded the coffee which tasted like soot. "What are you in the city for today?"

"Nothing, grandma thinks I am on a walk. I am usually gone for the whole day. But she'll be hungry soon."

"What does she like to eat?" George asked.

"She's fasting. It's a medical thing…" She looked out the window, playing with the knot on her scarf.

GOODNIGHT NOBODY

"Oh, surgery?" George sipped his drink. "Where do you go, all day?" He changed the subject, turning a glass of kombucha in his hand.

She shrugged.

"On the night we met, I am so sorry I was out of it. I don't remember even leaving, not the most gentlemanly." He scratched his head. "I usually don't get so wasted."

She nodded, holding back a grimace. The barista added a shot of pumpkin spice, which had no semblance to a real squash. "This will be an adventure."

A smile spread over George's face. "I brought my camping gear." He was drooling.

They walked to the car hand-in-hand from the shop to her parked car.

"Whoa! I didn't expect a convertible." George grazed the silver hood with his fingers. "Shouldn't you have a pick-up truck?"

"A friend let me borrow this." She smirked

RED'S OFFERINGS

and bowed at the vehicle. Sometimes, she didn't deserve the generosity of others.

***

George and Meredith drove the long way to Popo's house. Turning down a dirt path, rocked tinned against the rims and metal chassis. The car rocked in and out of potholes until the tires locked.

George scratched his head. "Triple-A doesn't can't help here. We'll have to walk back to the main road."

"Don't fuss. This is the perfect place to start." Meredith carried a small bag and an extra pillow while George strapped on an overflowing pack. He brought everything: waterproof clothing, food rations, water filter, solar panels, and an axe.

"I am ready." He surveyed the wooded area and grass growing from the path under his feet. Trees grew wild. "Backcountry, huh?"

They trudged through mire, taking quick breaks for snacks and flirting. When the day dimmed, George turned on his headlamp. "Are we meeting grandma today?"

"Not yet." She placed her finger on her lips.

George nodded.

At the campsite, a ring of stones encompassed a tent, two chairs, and an empty fire pit.

"A nice spot." He glanced at his phone.

"It's my happy place. No internet."

They chopped wood into small pieces then played games and sang songs around a fire. "No wonder, you grilled me about the outdoors. Cool first date."

Under the dark sky, they kissed. George took it slow, only touching her face.

"Wear this when you meet grandma." She tied a scarlet handkerchief around his wrist. "If she complains of indigestion then dissolve these antacids in her water."

"Do I need to protect myself from a little

RED'S OFFERINGS

old lady?" Wrinkled formed around his eyes in a joke.

"Old things are more vicious than you think." Meredith faked a laugh, being more honest than she had ever been. A cursed forced her to never say more. "You'll need your axe for more firewood." This would've sounded so weird with anyone else.

"Ah, yes. I will do my best to impress the matriarch. Most woman don't ask for weapons when meeting her family."

He was so nonchalant; she couldn't help to laugh. "I guess...I trust you enough." In the night, George couldn't see her touch a blade sheathed in the waist of her pants. Violence had a tendency to find her.

***

George woke up alone in the tent. Meredith left a note:

Follow the signs on the tree. Remember the firewood and antacids.

He brushed his teeth, changed his clothes,

GOODNIGHT NOBODY

and slicked back his hair. He double-checked the handkerchief and pocketed the medicine.

"What a thoughtful lady," he said out loud to the woods.

Grandmother's loved him. If firewood was requested, then firewood she shall get, even if it meant chopping down a tree. He followed markings on trunks. Hand drawn emojis of an axe, campfire, steak, a wolf, and a bloody knife. A joke? Meredith had reconstructed a woodland fairytale. He smiled at the romantic gesture.

Birds chirped. Happy to have a visitor. After ten minutes, smoke billowed from a chimney. On the ground, Meredith's boot prints lead him straight to the cabin. Dragging his axe in one hand, he climbed the stairs to the porch. Shivering as he smelled a stale stench. This wasn't the freshly baked cookies kind of grandmother. The small cabin was dingy.

A girl in a scarf was etched into the door. He knocked. "Hello, Grandma. I am Meredith's friend. I am here to…"

RED'S OFFERINGS

"Come in deary." A gruff voice answered.

As he pushed open the door, cigarette smoke and citrus hit his lungs. He coughed.

At the far end of the single roomed cabin, a figure overflowed in an armchair. Meredith's jacket crumpled on the ground made him second guess leaving the axe. She didn't seem to be the messy type. Walking inside, a fire burned in the hearth, an orange hue blanketed the room.

"Mmmm. This is an unexpected offering. Red…I mean Meredith insisted on no more friends." Grandma leaned back with an extended belly. "I shouldn't have been so hasty."

"Where's Meredith?" George gripped the wood axe handle, looking at the mustard carpet under grandma's bulging.

"She's out. And don't mind my sitting, gouts flared up." Grandma burped. "Pardon, too much for dinner."

He walked up to the table with a glass of water. It was only three o'clock. Dust clung

GOODNIGHT NOBODY

to every surface except for a small handprint on the clear glass of water. A sweaty and sour smell lingered in the air.

Grandma hiccupped.

"Here, try this for your discomfort." George showed Grandma the packet and poured white powder into the water. He stood back, searching for signs of Meredith. This could be a test. Or she was playing hide-and-seek.

"Why don't you stand near the fire? Don't want visitors to be cold." Grandma grabbed the drink and swallowed it whole. "That's much better. Why don't you sit down." She pointed a pudgy finger at a seat.

He politely refused.

Grandma grumbled then dipped long fingernails into a pot hanging over the flames. The flames casted grandma's skin in a dark gray. "This is chock full of vitamin C. Helps with swelling. Do you want some?" She sucked her fingers with a loud smack.

"I bet Meredith will be back any second.

RED'S OFFERINGS

Can you be a sweetie and get more antacids?" Grandma licked her lips with a thick tongue. "I want to be in tip top shape for conversation."

George picked up the empty cup and approached the sink.

Grandma grinned with a mouthful of teeth and burped. "Old age is gassy."

He turned his back to the fire as he filled the glass. But, out of the corner of his eyes, a shadow crept behind him. Bumps raised on his back as he felt something sharp press into the top of his head.

George rotated, smashing the glass against the side of a hairy head. A beastly screamed replaced his. Blood spilled onto the floor.

Watching am object protrude from Grandma's stomach, George grabbed the axe. Grandma shook then went limp. The mass continued to grow from her stomach.

"Ohhhh. Myyyy..." George raised up the axe with two hands as a head popped out then a neck and then a whole slender body. The person stared at him. A soiled cloth covering its hair.

"Wait." The newly appeared person waved.

George breathed hard through the smell of piss and blood.

"It's me. Meredith. Hurry, give me the axe." Her bloody footprints imprinted on the yellow and black rug. She swung the axe, chopping off grandma's paws. Panting and covered in goo, Meredith didn't stop. George observed in awe as she clamped a fiery log with tongs and placed it into the gaping wound. Grandma's face wasn't grandmotherly at all. It was a furry beast with a long snout and hollow eyes.

As a final act, Meredith dove under the bed. She and a white-haired person crawled out with no clothes. Meredith held her.

"This is not grandma. This is my Popo."

George snapped out of the shock. Gripping the exacted fur, he draped the new

RED'S OFFERINGS

skin around Popo.

LISTEN, BEFORE IT'S TOO LATE

Discomfort burned into the back of my neck, while I typed inside an empty house. I cranked the volume of a song that transmitted Amanda's spirit, *Sunday Kind of Love*. The rolling jazz muted creaking doors and groans. Sulphury scents impaled the room.

"Smudge," said friends, but I believed in faulty wiring and bad plumbing. The cat went missing yesterday.

As letters materialized in the steamy bathroom mirror, I felt her presence. I

LISTEN BEFORE IT'S TOO LATE

reached for my glasses and slipped on wet tiles. My foot rocketed upwards. I floated mid-air, facing the specter that tried to warn me of my impending death.

ON THE ISLE OF THE WILD

Queen Logan rules with her fists in the Isle of the Wild.

"BE STILL," she commands to the lion-headed dragons, peering into their pearl-shaped eyes. Beasts beat golden lashes against silken cheeks. They lower their heads with saliva dripping from their mouths.

"We love you so." The crowd shouts in their peculiar language. This means — *you can never leave*. The previous ruler had escaped in haste. Sailing to another world without a goodbye. These fantastical beasts

GOODNIGHT NOBODY

dislike disloyalty. They devoured traitors.

The Queen leaps from the throne with her cape studded with colorful gems. She strides through rows of hanging tongues. Her long hair trailing behind. Multi-colored manes hide terrible yellowed stares.

Eating the leader is against the rules.

As long as she wears the velvet crown, she is not fodder.

"BEGIN." Queen Logan waves her scepter atop the tallest tree. Shoelaces around the stick once sparkled with reds and blues. The colors of her basketball team who took the 1992 Junior High Basketball Championships.

Menacing grins focus on the movements of her hands. She taps the staff to commence the daily rumpus.

The long-tailed creatures stop licking their terrible lips and gnashing their terrible teeth. Instead, they dance their terrible awkward jigg. Drums beat in an uneven rhythm. Their bodies obstructing a possible path home.

RED'S OFFERINGS

As day fades, the decorated dragons twist and somersault and Queen Logan retires to a secret spot on the beach. She lays next to rotting wood planks and rusted nails, remnants belonging to a previous King. In the rubble, she is unseen by crazed golden eyes.

Her story is different than the fabled King who had sailed from a faraway land. An earthquake had shaken at the final basketball game, caving in the roof. Logan had ducked under the bleachers. She dragged her belly through wreckage into a tunnel. Thinking the heating duct would send her to the street, she crawled for a long time. At the other end was this isle.

Now, on the sand, she stretches her neck then squats in a perfect kung fu horse stance. Bending her knees in a ninety-degree angle, stacking them over her ankles. She holds the position until her thighs shake and collapse. Then it is time for the real training. Six-hundred kicks and fifteen dozen sets of punches during the waning phase. Tree climbing and pull-ups during the full moon.

GOODNIGHT NOBODY

Logan must stay ahead of drooling beasts. Each one is hungrier than the next. Yet like them, Queen Logan dreams about food — macaroni and cheese with baskets of steaming soup dumplings — and the people who had loved her the most. One day, she will find her way back.

GOODNIGHT NOBODY

THE VEGETARIAN

Pink blossomed on Dad's cheeks. The hue matched stitches of his grilling apron. "But, you ate meat yesterday?" He peaked into the cooler then pointed his tongs at the trees. "You better pray the forest has plans for your rumbling belly."

liiiickk, he wanted to reply. Jason shoved his hands into his pockets. He could swallow a few pieces of chicken, but this morning was tough. Reddish hairs poked out from the lumpy meat on the grill. "I am vegetarian."

GOODNIGHT NOBODY

Branches swayed at his lie.

"Do eight-year-olds even know what that means?" Dad huffed, rotating sausages cooking over coals. "This trip was your idea. Otherwise, I would be content and full of burgers in Florida." He stared dreamily up in the sky. The woods absorbed their conversation.

Jason shrunk deeper into his hoodie. Crammed into a motel room, the family fought. The forest preserve, he thought offered space. But they still confined their activities to the campsite and watched shows on screens.

Charred blistery skin on the sausage dangling from his father's tongs made Jason queasy.

"Anyone would kill for this super-premium breakfast. Ack. I am so hungry here." Dad's shoulder jerked in an aggressive shrug.

While grocery stores were miles away, woodland creatures didn't need pre-packaged foods. Jason didn't have internet to figure out what veggies ate for breakfast.

ON THE ISLE OF THE WILD

Salad?

"Hon. Don't be dramatic." Mom shouted from the tent. "Not everyone wants your stinky junk."

Dad pressed his lips together, wiping sweat from his brow. An oily aroma of pepper and garlic salted the air. Jason didn't move, distracted by the disgust rising in his throat.

"Eeekk." He jumped when his mom touched his arm.

"You're a ball of nerves." Her hair tumbled from the bun at top of her head. "Lamb chop. Plants eat meat too."

Jason hated food-based nicknames. Mom was being nice. He whispered, "I doubt Venus Fly Traps would bother with blood sausages." Meat stuffed into intestinal tubes.

"Carnivores aren't picky. They eat everything: flies, chipmunks, or whatever. Plants blend into surroundings and hunt by attracting victims with sweet smelling scents." Mom's look was intense.

GOODNIGHT NOBODY

She chuckles, patting him on the hand. "Don't look so terrified. I am trying to give you a perspective."

Jason relaxed. "Good thing I am not big."

Mom foisted a set of car keys into his hand. She smelled like roses. "Big enough to grab a bag from the trunk. It's filled with fruit."

Dad coughed, oblivious to their tangent.

"Don't blame your dad. He just cares and not well versed in persuasion. Sweeter is better. Just like you honey cakes." Mom pinched his cheeks. Even if she hadn't showered for three days, she still smelled like rose shampoo.

Jason smiled, hopping from the picnic table. He had a temporary escape. "I hope there are snacks too." He was relieved to forage from the car.

"Stick to the path. We don't want a fox to carry you away." Concern flashed on mom's face. She worried too much.

ON THE ISLE OF THE WILD

The parking lot was farther than Jason remembered. Except for school, he was hardly ever farther than a few blocks away from his parents. He trembled. He was alone, fending for himself at the edge of civilization. Fear gave way to excitement.

Freeeee. His heart sung.

The trunk was empty. Returning with nothing would subject him to more jokes. Jason was hungry enough to devour hairy sausages. Fennel seeds and ground meat stuffed into intestinal sacks made him want to barf. He stuck out his tongue. Breakfast was battle he wanted to win.

He checked the park map. They camped inside an old growth forest, where the trees had stood the same way for thousands of years.

Then, he spotted a squirrel across the paved lot, sniffing at the roots of an oak tree. He walked towards the small animal. A roasted tar scent filled the air. Closer, the squirrel's tail swung as it slurped up acorns. Shells crunched under his feet.

GOODNIGHT NOBODY

Jason picked up a nut, rolled the ball in his hand. He bites down with his back teeth. "Ouuchhhh." He was surprised. It wasn't easy, not eating meat.

The squirrel shot up, meeting Jason with its red eyes. Then it bolted into the dark forest. Leaves rustled overhead. As he rounded the tree, the sun dimmed, and shadows rose.

Nuts overflowed from his pockets. He could roast or grind them with mom's mortar and pestle.

Wheee. What a silly project. Nature was hard work. But his dad would appreciate his fortitude. He would reveal his vegetarian instincts.

The leaves changed from green to shades of grey. Strange noise echoed around him. He turned, around and around, trying to find the car. Trunks sliced the horizon into vertical bars. A tree, the sky, and then trees again.

"Heeeeelp." His shouts fell flat as tears roll down his cheek. He told himself he

ON THE ISLE OF THE WILD

couldn't be lost. Weighted down by acorns, he trudged in a direction he assumed was camp. Moss grew on the Northwest side of trees. Cardinal directions blurred under twisted branches and uneven ground. Was it him or were the trees getting angrier? Sweat soaked his Transformers shirt.

Then suddenly, he caught a floral scent. Joy exploded in his heart. Mom must be close. Why hadn't she come get him sooner? The aroma of apple cider spiced with cinnamon. Mom had the fruit bag after all. *Yippee.*

Thirst stoked his confusion. Where was the tent and grill? Had they packed up to leave? Dad mentioned being hungry, so were they ordering pizza?

"Dad, I am sorry I didn't eat breakfast." No one responded.

Hungry ignited his desperation. So, when he found a hammock affixed between the trees, he ran right into it. After all, only their SUV was parked in the lot.

The floating bed smelled oddly appetizing.

GOODNIGHT NOBODY

Grease ticked the inside of his nose. His father was teaching him a lesson. "Dad, I get it. I'll eat anything."

Jason touched the tiny hairs quivering on the fabric. They were sticky. Noises gurgled from inside the hammock's folds. "What? Did someone say something?" He put his ear very close to the opening, until he heard his name.

Yanking open the folds, a sugary smell bursted out. It smelled like blueberry jam and honey on toast. *Yaassssh.* His favorite breakfast of all time. He reached inside, squeezing a thing that felt like a memory-foam pillow. He was tired.

Without a fight, he crawled into the hanging pod. His parents or rangers would find him. He needed a nap. His legs landed into gelatinous blankets. A soothing voice coaxed him to close his eyes. Yet, one hand gripped onto lip of the hammock, refusing to let go. The hammock was made of a funny material, too rigid to be fabric. He sank deeper into a mesmerizing spell.

Jason was in a dream, sleeping inside of

ON THE ISLE OF THE WILD

his tent. Mom called his name. Sounds faded as his ears filled with fluid. For a minute, he swam in a viscous vat. Warmth coated his bare skin, squeezing out his strength. Acorns tumbled from his pockets, drifting upwards towards a sliver of light. He couldn't feel his arms and legs or else he would've chased after the treasures.

Elation transformed to an ache. The water was dyed red. Full-bodied flavor seeped into his mouth. His eyes slowly sealed shut. For a second, he realized the stew was of his own flesh. The flavor was perfect, absolutely delicious. Plants eat meat, mom already told him.

THE THING ABOUT CHEESE

What does a mouse eat?

Gooey cheese smeared under a trap's tension spring.

    With a single lick, the bar snaps, breaking its furry neck.

            Was it a delicious nibble?

What does her baby eat?

    The mother while she still twitches.

THE THING ABOUT CHEESE

Starting at the nails, baby is shy. Nibbling until a trickle of blood emboldens the little darling's appetite. It moves to the soft stomach. Sharp teeth slices open the skin, spilling intestines stuffed with grass, breadcrumbs, and stolen pantry things. A flavorsome sausage spread without remorse. The child doesn't eat alone. It binges and then dies from thirst.

Worth every hungry bite?

BORN OF THE BLOOD MOON: BEFORE THE FROG SANG FROM THE WELL

When the earth thirsted for light, the sky birthed a tiny creature named Shuja. A mass of stars landed onto rain-drenched moss. Noise fell away until the blood moon's child drew its first breath. The ground nestled the guest between earthen walls, cradling it with pulverized bark.

Bald and crimson, Shuja yawned, unknowing its purpose. The darkness promised a beast's terror. The forest paid tribute, offering carcasses and viscera to nurture its cravings of blood.

"Rise up!" The wolves howled. Rodents

GOODNIGHT NOBODY

whispered ancient stories to the shapeless thing, begging it to sharpen its teeth.

From the depths of a hole, Shuja followed the clouds. "How wonderful to gaze at the bright sky." It giggled as bugs wrapped its body tight with silk strands.

The worms warned it of the dreadful things above ground. "Here, you are safe. Stay with us."

"My heart summons me higher. Don't worry I shall return." It busted from the larva and squirmed up the shaft. Its skin shining under the moonlight, a bird witnessed the morsel emerging, snatching it between its beak.

"Will you eat me?" Shuja cried as talons squeezed tighter. The bird dropped her into a nest filled with squealing chicks. Growing large with its wings, the bird swooped away and returned with a mouse.

"Who are you?" hooted the bird as its claws ripped through the rodent.

"I am an earthworm." Shuja beamed. The

mother regurgitated pieces of flesh into each of her babes.

The bird blinked brilliant yellow eyes and passed meat to Shuja. "You are too shiny to be a worm."

Shuja ate greedily, cuddling with her found brothers and sisters.

The moon child sprouted wings and learned to hone into the rustling of leaves. Adventure sighed from the mountains. Shuja was the last to soar beyond the canopy. With the wind against decadent plumage, it took to the open skies; it glided over snow-covered peaks, drinking from the rapids and inhaling the clouds. The earthbound creature absorbed nature's rite.

One sunny afternoon, a large furry brute stumbled upon Shuja in the water. "This is my river."

Shuja approached the four-legged brawn without fear.

"What are you?" The bear was soon distracted by soft caresses on its belly,

GOODNIGHT NOBODY

intoxicated by a heavenly scent.

Shuja nuzzled a hairless head into the bear's chest. "I am an owl," it said in a coo.

The bear's furred mouth tumbled with laughter. "But you have no feathers on your wings." It licked Shuja's face and electricity pulsated inside and became one with the earthly creature. For months, they basked in the fields and caught fish on the river's bank. In autumn colors shifted. In the final warmth of the year, Shuja expanded with life.

Curling up in a cave as snow fell, it snuggled close with offspring sprung from its loins. Shuja's milk and celestial blood nourished them. It howled as the brood ventured away the following season. Her babies were full-grown.

One day, Shuja strolled beyond the mountains into a new valley. Barren fields surrounded a house. People walked on two limbs, covered from head to toe. It listened to the hum of voices through open windows which roused the feeling of thorns rubbing against its skin. Yet, it was curious about the creatures who rode horses, squeezed milk

BORN OF THE BLOOD MOON

from bovines, and bounced babies on their knees.

So, Shuja shook off the fur, bite off its nails, and fashioned a suit out of leaves. It wobbled standing on two legs.

When it knocked on the door, a mousy voice asked, "Who's there?"

Shuja's throat tightened, morphing grunts into words. "Me neighbor. Bear." It had longed for a connection.

By now the story of a creature born during the last blood moon had carried far. Spreading wide were warnings of werewolves, vampires, and monsters part insect, bird, and giant. Shuja had brought forth the moon god's wrath, her children with silver skin, three eyes, and flightless wings mad humans trembled in the darkness.

"You're not a bear, just a girl. Come in for tea." A man and woman laughed with twisted grins, knowing only greed and wickedness towards this crimson girl with glistening skin. This fabled creature could fetch a generous sum. So, the woman

GOODNIGHT NOBODY

oozed hospitality and the man sprinkled purple petals into a cup of tea drink.

The more tea Shuja sipped, the heavier its eyes grew, and slowly its head lowered onto the table.

Shuja awoke in a drafty barn. Its limbs were bound, and teeth knocked out. With no claws, it could not cut the ties. The humans had gone to fetch the highest bidder. It howled and stomped, summoning its world: worms burrowed from underground tunnels, birds severed the restraints, and its beastly children extracted a blood thirsty revenge.

Beasts, small and large, feasted on flesh and bones. As the lore foretold, no woman could hold back the beasts because greed tasted fragrant, and death blossomed a new order.

Village by village packs scorched fields, freed livestock, and trampled homes. The beasts' appetites burgeoned until nothing could quell their urges.

Until one morning, Shuja peered into a pit lined with flowers. It recalled the wisdom of the worm. When Shuja first descended, it longed for nothing. While the night pleaded for violence, the moon's child shrank and retired to the one view of the world, peace.

The myth of the moon beasts faded, overgrown by weeds and ferns. Moss blanketed Shuja's iridescent skin. Time drowned the fears lingering in human memories, never stopping to ask the not-so-ignorant creature. Why is the bottom of a well to be such a wondrous place to live and see the world?

AUTHOR NOTES

1. **Goodnight Nobody**: First published in Duck Duck Mongoose. I memorized *Goodnight Moon* within a few months of bedtime duties. The last few pages lingered in my mind. So, after falling headfirst into cosmic horror, I leaned into my questions about the knitting old lady and Nobody.

2. **A Wicked Spice**: First published in Friday Flash Fiction. My first micro-fiction were entered into a contest. I didn't win, but it opened my world to tiny fiction.

3. **Red's Offerings**: Red becomes her own Final Girl. She doesn't have to wait for the hunter to save her. Reinforcements are and distractions are nice.

4. **Listen, Before It's Too Late**: First published in 101 words. A friend sees a ghost, another writes it down. No death in real life.

4. **On the Isle of the Wild**: A top ranked hit at bedtime. Mischievous Max in the story stole my heart. The island didn't disappear after he sailed away. Logan means small.

5. **The Vegetarian**: Food preferences change. Food preferences change. Nature is adaptable.

7. **The Thing About Cheese** - Since returning home to carnage, I have been thinking about the field mice trapped in our basement – a mom and a baby. RIP.

8. **Born of the Blood Moon: Before the Frog Sang from the Well** – <u>Published in Space and Time Magazine</u>. This is an origin story for the Chinese fable The Frog in the Well. This questions the frog's ignorance. The creature deserves to be heard. I remind myself often -- I am enough. Society conditions us to doubt our authenticity. Validation doesn't come from the outside. Stop over valuing external knowledge over your own perspectives. Rest in your power.

ABOUT THE AUTHOR

Pauline Chow writes speculative fiction to explore alternative histories and possible futures. She lives in the woods and is planning her next trip to a historical (hopefully haunted) hotel. Not your average techie, she used to sue slumlords and advocate for affordable housing in Southern California. But her love of snow brought her back to the Midwest. Her words appear in Cosmic Horror Monthly, APOCALYPSE CONFIDENTIAL, Duck Duck Mongoose, 101 words, and more forthcoming.

LET'S CONNECT

Author Website:
https://paulinechowstories.com/

Subscribe for Updates:
https://paulinechow.substack.com/

X:
www.x.com/@itspaulinechow/

Instagram:
www.instagram.com/@paulinechowstories/

Made in the USA
Middletown, DE
04 July 2024